D0293529

TIMACK
CREATIONS

VERONA

BENEDICT ASHFORTH

VERONA

Benedict Ashforth

Copyright 2015 by Patrick O'Neill

Benedict Ashforth can be contacted at
benedict2012@hotmail.co.uk

Edited by Nikki O'Neill & Patrick Hargan

*With special thanks to Nikki for always being there
when I delve into the madness*

This is dedicated to Iain Angus Forsythe
We miss you always

"HE IS FILLED WITH FURY, FOR HE KNOWS HIS TIME IS SHORT."

REVELATION 12:12

INTRODUCTION

St Mary's Church
Tyneham
Isle of Purbeck
Dorset

13 January 1991

Dear Mrs Andrews,

I have agonised over many weeks about whether or not I should send this to you. Ultimately, after the greatest struggle of conscience and reason, I have concluded that a far greater harm may befall should I not.

Given all that has taken place, I have no doubt you will find its content extremely upsetting. In truth, I have barely slept a night through since reading it myself. Please know that it is not my intention to cause you further distress.

What follows is Charles Carter's account. He sent it to me six months ago and it has been a heavy burden, I will admit. At times I have considered destroying it, condemning it to the flames, but I have always stopped myself at the last. I believe there is a great deal at stake here.

Everything he has written is true, so far as the physical elements are concerned. I have seen first-hand the church of San Lorenzo in Verona and the ruins described later on. As for the other, more unsettling elements, it is for you to decide and interpret as you see fit.

Please forgive the most unspeakable inference made in my sending this to you, which will make itself clear as you read. I only pray you understand that my decision was born of goodwill and nothing more.

Yours sincerely,

Father Henry Stephens

CHARLES CARTER'S ACCOUNT

Creech Lane Cottage
Creech
Isle of Purbeck
Dorset

24 July 1990

Father Henry,

You will understand soon enough why I have sent this. All I ask is that you keep it safe and pass it to whoever may need it, when the time is right.

You are a religious man, but I warn you, you will find in this matter — as I did — that God alone is not enough. I advise you to read this on a bright day and not as shadows gather. They say the half-light plays tricks on the eye, but there will be no illusion here, only hard truth, and I implore you to stay in the open, where the comfort of others can be relied upon.

And so I will begin — but not at the start. We were not even born then. No, I will begin at the hospital five months ago, in the consulting room of the Nuffield Fertility Clinic, where it began for us, where our chapter started.

'Take some time off work. Get away somewhere different. You both look shattered.'

He was right, of course. After five excruciating

years of failed IVF treatments, we now faced the bleak reality we had always feared: a future without our own children.

We sat for an eternity as Mr Edwards slipped our records neatly into a filing cabinet, consigning the chronicles of our unsuccessful endeavours to darkness forever.

Though Caroline was silent, I knew she was screaming inside. It is different for women, although I do not pretend to understand. The loss is fundamental – primal – and more painful than a blade cutting through nerve. She maintained her composure, but her face told its own, harrowing story. We were being forced to abandon something irreplaceable, to simply leave it behind, but what exactly? Our hopes? Our ideals? Our dreams? Or something else entirely? A part of me understood exactly how she felt. How do you replace something that never existed? How do you grieve for the child that never lived, and never died?

She had taken the pregnancy test, but we had clung to the remote possibility that the consultant would tell us something different, just once, just this final time. Hope is a strange thing, Father, is it not? However small and insignificant it appears, we grasp at it until the very end. At least, that is how I used to be. I know better now. Some things cannot be controlled. Some outcomes are unalterable. Some fates are set in stone.

We had met at Oxford University in the winter of 1970. I was reading Philosophy, Politics and Economics at Brasenose and Caroline was taking an English degree at St Anne's, a subject that would eventually lead her to a career in teaching. I first saw her at a failed dinner party at James Corcoran's small Victorian house on the Iffley Road. James and I had become friends since meeting in freshers' week. We shared an interest in music and women, though in truth neither of us had had much luck since arriving in Oxford. James would often hold parties, inviting as many people as he could on the premise that eventually his fortune would turn. In the end it was my destiny that was changed that night, not his.

I remember the snow that evening. Thick snow, swirling about the street lights, settling easily on the frozen pavements as I made my way across Magdalen Bridge, towards my destination. An icy wind bit at my face as I turned on to Iffley Road and made my way closer. I passed the track where Roger Bannister had cracked the four-minute mile. It was indistinguishable from the road in the whiteness.

I'm not sure how long I stood at the door, waiting for James to answer. It seemed like an eternity standing there in the cold. Then I heard a woman's voice behind me.

'Hello?'

I turned to see Caroline stepping up from the darkened street. She wore a blue duffle coat and a pink scarf. Her eyes were bright and green against porcelain features. Locks of dark hair fell about her face as she smiled. My heart stopped. People talk of love at first sight. I had never thought it possible until that moment in the snow outside James's front door. The amber glow from the street lights illuminated her soft skin. She was the most beautiful thing I had ever seen.

Later, we discovered that James had cancelled the dinner. His father had been taken ill in London and he had left by train to Paddington to be at his side. We were the only ones not to have been told.

To escape the cold, we found a quiet corner in the nearby Half Moon pub and talked the evening away over beer and cigarettes. My conversation was stilted and awkward because, every time I looked at her, I was transfixed once again by her beauty.

So began our fated journey together. We graduated in the summer of 1973 and had moved to a flat in Reading by the end of the same year. I worked in London and Caroline took a position teaching English at a local school. We never liked the city life and always dreamt of a quieter existence in the fresh air, but still we endured it, first in Reading and then, much later, in Southampton.

We were married at the small chapel at Englefield, Berkshire, on 20 December 1980. Caroline's father was still alive then, and so gave her away to me. How wonderful she looked.

Even now I remember it as though it were just moments ago: her small hand in mine, white lace across her face, the taste of her lips on mine. Her knowing smile as she whispered, 'I do.'

We had it all ahead of us.

We dreamt of having a family from the start.

****

We drove back to Creech Lane Cottage in silence, through the barren Purbeck valleys where rugged ponies stood motionless against gun-metal skies. The first droplets of rain began to fall as we passed Tyneham and, as we climbed the narrow road that led away from the village, a bird of prey swooped in front of the car, winging ahead, as though leading our way home.

I glanced at Caroline.

She stared blankly through the windscreen at the road. Her face was half-hidden behind dark locks, but not enough to conceal the tears. I reached out and squeezed her hand.

We had considered fostering, adoption and surrogacy. It was the main reason we had bought the house just two months earlier. Whatever happened, we had decided, we would have children one way or another. And here, at Creech Lane Cottage, we would have all the room we needed to raise them. The directorship at Elliot Thorpe Financial that I had landed the previous year, at age forty, had enabled us to make the move to the countryside, from our cluttered flat in Southampton.

Now, with Caroline's income as a primary school teacher in neighbouring Wareham, we lived in comfort, with a healthy disposable income, for the first time in our lives. All that was missing was the one thing we yearned for most. Other than identifying mild scar tissue on Caroline's ovarian tubes, the doctors had found nothing. They simply labelled it 'unexplained infertility'.

We had agreed that, if we were unsuccessful with IVF this last time, we would start the adoption process. But now, as the car rumbled and jerked down the potholed driveway of Creech Lane Cottage, this notion seemed a million miles away.

I parked near the front door and Caroline went straight inside without looking back, leaving me alone with the steady ticking of rain. As I sat behind the wheel, deflated and confused, I could not ignore the feeling that we had lost ourselves in all this. The weeks, months and hours of waiting patiently for failed test results were finally over and now, faced with this truth, we had become strangers, driven apart from each other in our fruitless quest.

Through the windscreen, the sandstone structure was solemn against the heavy skies, its receding windows black and uninviting. It was my frame of mind, I suppose, but I had never viewed the house in this way before. It was as grave and desolate as we were.

How different it had been when we had first seen the place. On that day, Creech Lane Cottage had been bright and impressive: sunlit Purbeck stone against clear blue skies, exactly what we had been looking for. Caroline fell in love with it immediately. Tucked away from civilisation, hidden in the unfarmed hills of the Jurassic Coast, and only a few miles from the forgotten village of Tyneham and your beloved church, Father Henry, the cottage was the perfect escape from city life that we had been searching for. As the Ministry of Defence controls much of the countryside, few properties are bought and sold here. The landscape will not change.

The young agent from Emerson Briars had

explained that the previous owners, Mr and Mrs Hawthorn, had lived in the house for less than a year before the bank foreclosed, repossessing the property in the process. The Hawthorns had haemorrhaged every penny into knocking through walls and rebuilding the kitchen and dining areas in an attempt to update the structure. Then Mr Hawthorn, an executive with a local insurance firm, was made redundant halfway through the work. The dominoes began to fall.

Eager to liquidate their security without delay, the bank procured the services of Emerson Briars to sell the house at a reduced price. Through my contacts, and as first viewers of the property, we offered the full asking price, which was agreed instantly.

As often in life, Father, one man's loss becomes another man's gain, and so it was with us and the Hawthorns, or so I believed.

'What do you think,' I said, as we lay in bed that evening. 'About taking a trip, getting away from it all, like the doctor said?'

'It wouldn't change anything, Charlie.'

'I'm not saying it would, but the move has been exhausting, and now all of this again. We could relax. Take some time for each other. Look, I'll take you wherever you like.'

Outside, a cow moaned through the silence, echoing for miles across the fields.

When Caroline spoke, a cloud obscured the moon. The room fell into darkness.

'Italy.'

Then I felt it for the first time; something different, almost beyond perception but every bit as real as the word Caroline had spoken. Yes, it was there already, surely, that distant but unmistakable sense of dread, building steadily as the seconds passed.

A chill ran down my spine as she spoke again, partly because I thought she had fallen asleep in those tense moments, but it was more than that. I saw her mouth move, but her voice was unfamiliar, as though belonging to someone else. A child perhaps, whispering.

'Verona.'

Then she was asleep.

****

The following morning I drove to Wareham and ransacked the local travel agencies for all the Italian short-break glossies I could find. Caroline was still sleeping when I returned and so, before leaving for Bournemouth, I displayed them neatly across the kitchen table, each one open at the Verona section, to surprise her when she finally came downstairs.

Apart from its famous Shakespearean connection, I knew nothing of the place. Caroline had never travelled there either and, although it was an unusual choice, it felt right. What could be more enticing than escaping the rain and misery to explore an Italian city that neither of us knew? Bring me sunshine…

'Great idea, Charles,' said Hugo, closing his office door and offering me a seat. 'God knows you both deserve a rest. Beautiful city, Verona. It'll be nice and warm this time of year, too. Get to the lake if you can. It's only an hour or two to Garda on the bus. Coffee?'

'No, thank you.'

As managing director, Hugo Thorpe was the only individual in a position to authorise my absence at such short notice, and I had worked with him for long enough to know that conditions would be attached to his agreement.

'Listen,' he continued, taking a seat and resting

his slender hands on the desk. 'I know you've been through it lately and I have absolutely no issue with you taking holiday, God forbid, but we must – how shall I say – leave the house in order.'

He caught me with his keen grey eyes.

'Where are we with the Webber case?'

Maurice and Margo Webber had been referred to us by Lacey and Stockwell Solicitors on completion of their recently updated wills and powers of attorney. Like many people their age, the Webbers were looking for advice about inheritance tax because of their sizeable assets, which, taking into account the money in the bank and their unencumbered property, brought them well into the realm of significant liability. In fact, the two million pounds held in cash from the disposal of their foreign property would have put them in this position all on its own.

One of my colleagues had visited them, and I was aware that we had issued a recommendation report. This outlined our advice to set up a discretionary trust that would eventually benefit the Webbers' grandchildren and, assuming that the Webbers survived for more than seven years, cancel their tax liability in its entirety.

On receipt of the report, the Webbers had contacted the office with a number of questions, and it had been decided that, in my capacity as director, I should arrange a meeting to help them understand the workings of the proposed trust in more depth – and, of course, pick up the two-million-pound cheque, one and a half per cent of which would then belong to the firm.

'I have a meeting with them tomorrow night,' I lied. 'At their home in Burley.'

The previous week, my thoughts had been only of Caroline, and our hopes of a future filled with our own children. The Webbers could not have been further from my mind.

'I'm glad to hear it. You're exactly right for this, Charles. Not just anyone can deal with this kind of thing, you know. It would be nice to' – he paused to raise an eyebrow – 'conclude matters before you disappear?'

It wasn't a question, but a polite way of saying, 'I want the two-million-pound cheque in my hand before you leave the country.'

'I'll close it, Hugo,' I said evenly. 'Leave it with me.'

Later, at Creech Lane Cottage, I noticed that only one travel brochure now lay on the kitchen table. I called out for Caroline, but there was no answer. I opened it at the page that she had dog-eared, and smiled to myself as I saw the scribbled asterisk beside her selection: Hotel Galilei. It was four-star and expensive but, centrally located as it was, and tucked away in a leafy side street, it looked perfect.

My heart sank as I saw the handwritten note beside the brochure:

Charlie,

I'm sorry. I'm staying with Sarah for the next few days. I need to clear my head. I'll be back on Friday morning. I love you. Call if you need me. Sorry.

C x

Although I had nothing against Caroline's decision to spend some time with her sister – far from it – all the same, I couldn't help feeling undermined in some way. Could she not talk to me? Was I not enough? I had always thought that the experiences we had shared over the past twenty years had brought us closer together. But now I couldn't have felt further away from her.

In truth, I had never liked Sarah. Pathetic jealousy, I suppose you would call it. Being an only child with long-dead parents, I resented sharing Caroline, however seldom it was, and especially with Sarah. Where Caroline was loving and kind, Sarah was hard, controlling and ambitious. Perhaps we were too similar, Sarah and I. Perhaps she felt the same jealousy and resentment as I did. After all, her parents were dead too, and all she had now, as I did, was Caroline.

Still, I considered, screwing up the note and throwing it in the kitchen bin, it would give me time to organise the Italian trip and, of course, deal with the Webbers.

Once I had located our passports in an unpacked box, I booked flights for the coming Saturday, returning Tuesday, and then rang ahead to the hotel to make reservations. The receptionist spoke fluent English, which was a relief, and, an hour later, having organised travel insurance and ordered currency to collect from the airport, plus a few extras, I rang the Webbers and agreed to meet them the following evening, just as I had told Hugo.

****

The Webber residence was a large Georgian affair, with tall windows and a neatly trimmed, reddening creeper that covered the entire face of the house. The gravelled driveway, flanked by ancient cedars, ran straight up to the front door and, as I approached, a herd of fallow deer grazing in the shadows turned with anxious suspicion.

I wasn't nervous in the slightest about answering questions or collecting cheques. I had been in this situation so often that, as I parked the car and stepped on to the driveway, it felt more like an inconvenience than a challenge. Soon I would be in Verona with Caroline, far from any of this.

Just remain focused, I told myself, just for this one, final task. Be positive. Adapt. Connect. Control.

Before I had a chance to ring the bell, Mr Webber opened the door and stepped into the light. He stooped and there seemed to be something wrong with his right foot, which bent at an odd angle, but, as he stared up at me and smiled, his bright blue eyes shone with surprising energy from a tanned face framed by wild grey hair.

'Ah, the young Mr Carter.'

'Please,' I said, shaking his frail hand. 'Call me Charlie.'

'Then Charlie it shall be. Come on in and meet

Margo.'

Though spacious, the reception area was unfurnished save for a frayed burgundy carpet spread over the flagstones, and it didn't surprise me that the overhead chandelier was unlit. The elderly have a different perspective from the young when it comes to saving energy, or economy of any kind for that matter. They have known harder times, when saving and rationing were keys to survival. The Webbers were no exception.

'Just through here.' Mr Webber hobbled through an oak partition and into the main house. 'We'll use the table so we can all sit down.'

I followed him through a library where leather-bound books were arrayed in perfect formation from skirting to cove, and then through a sliding door into the dining room, where a polished mahogany table stretched out beneath high, leaded windows. Again, there was no overhead lighting, nor was there a need for it. The late afternoon sunlight that spilt across the extensive lawns outside cast a bright glow about the wood panelling. A grandfather clock ticked away the seconds in the corner of the room.

'Take a seat, Charlie.'

He ushered me to the table where the Elliot Thorpe recommendation report sat beside a jug of iced water and three glasses.

'Extraordinary place,' I said.

'We are lucky, yes. It's peaceful here, though perhaps a bit too big for us now. It's the upkeep, you see. Twenty years ago I managed it all myself. Now we have to rely on gardeners and cleaners and such like to keep it all ticking over. Still, a small price to pay for comfort, I always think. Ah, here's Margo now.'

Despite her years, Mrs Webber was an elegant creature. She wore a light-pink silk blouse that draped about her slender wrists, and her greying hair was tied neatly into a bun. Her large, dark eyes gave her an elfin appearance and she wore a gentle, regal smile that made me feel at ease immediately.

We shook hands and sat opposite each other as Maurice took the head of the table and rubbed his palms together.

'Right then, let's begin, shall we?'

Mr Webber had a raft of questions about the workings of the trust and the underlying investments. He listened carefully to my answers and jotted down notes as I explained.

'So you see,' I said, 'not only will the assets pass to your grandchildren and fall outside of your estate for inheritance-tax purposes, but you can also expect a decent growth on your investments over and above inflation. We'll spread the monies through a number of asset classes, to reduce risk and ensure that you're protected against the failure of a single holding. In essence, by spreading the monies in this way, over many areas, you reduce risk through diversification and···'

As I continued, I noticed that Mrs Webber hadn't said a word since the meeting had begun, but stared at me with an odd, faraway expression. I continued regardless, occasionally glancing in her direction while I outlined the in-house investment strategy and quarterly rebalancing process. When I had finished, Mr Webber nodded.

'Well, you've certainly been very clear and helpful. Hasn't he, Margo?'

'Yes,' she said absently. 'Very concise. Thank you.'

'Right, where do we sign, Charlie?'

The rest was simple. A swift completion of standard trust documents with myself as witness, an offshore investment-bond application and, of course, the collection of a cheque to the tune of two million pounds. I had connected, as I knew I would, and come through to the other side, only vaguely aware now of Mrs Webber's strange mood.

Within minutes I had shaken their hands and was sitting inside the car, leafing through the paperwork. Everything was in order: signed applications with passport details and particulars of wealth source; client and fee-agreement authorisations and copies of bank statements. Finally the cheque itself, inked in Mr Webber's fine hand, fully completed, but without signature. Damn it.

'Apologies, Charlie. I don't write cheques like this too often, you understand. Do come back through. Margo was just talking about you actually.'

The light had dimmed in the dining area and Mrs Webber stood gazing out over the lawns. She turned as I entered the room.

'I'm sorry to have been impolite this evening, Mr Carter,' she said. 'I haven't meant it to be that way. The truth is – '

'The truth is,' Mr Webber broke in, 'that, well, especially in situations like these – meetings, I mean – Margo can sometimes have… how can I put this now? Feelings.'

'Feelings?'

'I see things one normally would not see.'

'Margo has a gift. A psychic talent, if you will. It shows its face occasionally, but don't be alarmed. It comes and goes. Now, let's get that cheque signed and you can be on your way.'

'I see a child, Mr Carter.'

I almost laughed then, given what Caroline and I had been through in the past three years.

'That's not possible. I can't –'

'I understand your predicament.' Her voice was level and void of emotion. 'I do not speak of a baby, but of a child.'

My heart sank then. There was no way she could have known. The fine hairs on my neck stood on end and a cold silence settled over the room, broken only by the heavy ticking of the grandfather clock.

'The boy is here,' she said. 'As we speak.'

I tried to ignore it, the impossible idea that we were no longer alone, but I could not. Something had changed. Something tangible had altered in the room that I could not place, but it was every bit as genuine as Mrs Webber's voice.

I glanced at Mr Webber, who was hunched over, gripping the back of a chair with white knuckles.

'No,' Mrs Webber whispered. 'No, please.'

She was staring at something behind me, towards the door. Her features were ashen now and her large eyes wide with horror.

I tried to turn but could not. Something was close behind me. I knew it instinctively and yet, as I willed my body to move, it would not. I could only stare at Mrs Webber as she staggered backwards and thumped against the window pane.

'Margo!' He hobbled to her side as she slipped to the floor.

Her eyes rolled white. She twitched and trembled in Mr Webber's arms, pointing to the door behind me. Saliva trickled down her chin.

'*Raga*…' she croaked. '*Ragazzo.*' And then she fell limp.

I rushed over but Mr Webber raised a large hand.

'Stay where you are. She'll be fine, just give her a minute.'

Sure enough, she did come around, slowly, breathing heavily as he propped her in a dining-room chair and filled a glass of water.

'Should I call an ambulance?'

'There's no need. It comes and goes. Everything will be fine. Take the cheque and go, Charlie. And thank you for all your help. Please accept my apologies.'

I thanked him and turned to leave but, as I did, Mrs Webber spoke out.

'It's not right, Mr Carter,' she said quietly. 'It's all wrong.'

She was crying.

****

I thought little of the Webbers over the coming days. Perhaps I chose not to. In my mind the case was closed as surely as the cheque had now cleared through the bank. Hugo was pleased and I had no intention of upsetting Caroline with details of the occurrence, especially since she had returned from Sarah's in higher spirits than when she had left. In any case, what was there to tell? That an old woman had taken a strange turn?

The journey to Verona passed without incident. I had selected an expensive airline in order that our passage would be less arduous. No queues, along with access to the executive lounge, meant we could start relaxing immediately.

On board the half-empty plane, Caroline took the window seat and we watched the sun descend into the clouds far below, leaving a hellish skyscape of deep crimson in its wake. We kissed and held hands. In those moments, with that awesome spectacle of nature stretching out over the Alps, our sense of loss was palpable.

We landed safely in darkness at Villafranca and navigated the bustling arrivals hall to finally procure a taxi outside. The air was warm but comfortable and, as we sped along unfamiliar motorways and then through the darkened streets of Verona, bursts of

Italy shone through the night: a group of elderly men laughing in the greenish glow of a cafe bar; an ancient, floodlit bridge reflected in dark waters; a stray dog sniffing about an unlit alley.

The taxi bumped and jarred along a cobbled street before suddenly halting beside a set of bold, brass-handled doors.

'It's beautiful,' Caroline said, as we entered the hotel, and it was wonderful because, in that moment, I saw that she had momentarily forgotten our troubles and was, well, Caroline again.

The mahogany reception desk sat beneath an impossibly high, domed ceiling adorned with a fresco of Verona, painted in grey and gold, and complete with a pale depiction of Juliet at her balcony. The marble floors were furnished intermittently with deep red carpet, and an ancient-looking iron lift stood solidly beside the staircase.

Caroline sat in an ornate, upholstered armchair and gazed at the ceiling as I checked us in.

'Your room is on the third floor,' the receptionist said. Her accent was gentle and friendly, but she was most definitely in charge. 'Suite eleven.'

I noticed the neat row of guest books lined up in chronological order on the shelf behind her, each maroon volume embossed with its year in gold along the spine. The earliest was dated 1923.

'Enjoy your stay.' She smiled, revealing a fine set of white teeth, and waved to the porter who had already retrieved our cases from the taxi.

He was young, with jet-black hair, and immaculately presented in Hotel Galilei uniform.

'Sir,' he said. 'Please follow. I am sorry, but the lift is broken.'

We followed him upstairs to a small corridor on the third floor. Caroline smiled at me with nervous excitement as he put down our cases and opened the door to the suite.

'For me?' Caroline said, as she crossed the threshold.

It was just as I had planned. Lilac freesias and cream roses. The flowers of our wedding day, nine and a half years ago. The scent was extraordinary.

'Of course.'

She kissed me and strolled around the room, smiling and breathing in the sweet smell. The room itself was huge. Marbled walls and ceilings. The biggest bed I had ever seen in a hotel.

'It is beautiful,' Caroline said, turning to the porter. 'But is it possible to see a different one?'

'Yes, of course. We have one more suite left. I will show.'

It was unlike Caroline, but I went along with it and said nothing. I wanted her to feel completely at ease.

The next room, also on the third floor, was bigger still. With its stained-glass partition separating the living area from the bedroom and tall windows overlooking the small street below, I recognised it immediately as the room from the brochure.

'Stanza del Ragazzo Tranquillo,' the porter announced.

'This is it,' Caroline said absently. 'This is it exactly. Thank you.'

'I am so glad. I will bring the flowers and cases.'

Once I had tipped him and we were alone, Caroline held me tightly.

'Thank you so much,' she whispered. 'Everything is so wonderful.'

I left her to get changed and headed downstairs to the bar. On my way, I overheard the receptionist speaking in a hushed, irate tone. I understood little, but I picked out a few words: 'Ragazzo Tranquillo' and then, '*stupido*'.

That night, Caroline looked as elegant and beautiful as ever. She had chosen a loose-fitting dress, dark against her pale skin, that perfectly accentuated her slender form. We wandered out into the warm Italian night, taking everything in. Further along the narrow cobbled street where the hotel was located, we passed a small bar, illuminated by lanterns dangling among tendrils of ivy. A group of old men sat outside playing cards in the dimness, puffing at cigars and chuckling to themselves. One looked up at Caroline and nodded with approval as we passed. Mopeds ridden by young Italians sped by, weaving in and out of pedestrians and beeping as they went.

Further along, I led Caroline beneath an archway that opened onto another, darker alleyway: Vicolo Listone. Light bulbs, suspended from wires overhead, lit our way as we walked past a small, decrepit hotel.

Then, from the dimness, a glow emerged ahead: a restaurant, its square tables neatly aligned on the cobbles and dressed with red and white linen. It was busy, and the sweet aroma of fresh garlic and baked fish grew steadily stronger as we approached. A small sign on the crumbling wall of the alley announced: 'Ristorante Capra Nera'.

A tall waiter with long, dark hair and a welcoming smile strode over to where we stood.

'Good evening. Welcome. You have a reservation?'

'Are you Stefano?'

He nodded, causing locks to fall momentarily about his face.

'We spoke on the phone. The name's Carter.'

'Ah, yes. The special couple. I remember, of

course.'

'I apologise, we're early,' I said. 'I wasn't sure if the plane would be delayed or –'

'Early is perfect. This way, please.'

'Well, you have been busy, haven't you?' Caroline whispered as we followed Stefano in and around other diners to our table. 'Oh, my God.'

Stefano had not disappointed. A single vase: cream roses and lilac freesias; petals scattered across the table; prosecco on ice. He had given us the best table, at the edge of Vicolo Listone, overlooking the main piazza and the floodlit ruins of the ancient amphitheatre, Arena di Verona. It was exquisite.

I remember little of what was said that evening. Every now and then a warm breeze stole across the piazza, sending rose petals dancing and candles shimmering. We ate seafood and watched tiny figures meander around the crumbling gates of the amphitheatre. It was out of season and the crowds had not yet descended on the city, but it was still fairly busy.

I do remember one thing Caroline said, though.

'You need to relax, too. You've done so much to make this incredible, but you need to stop now, Charlie. Stop organising. Stop trying to control. Just be.'

In the candlelight, her features were smooth porcelain, just as they had been outside James Corcoran's house in Oxford, in the snow, all those years ago. Her green eyes shone as she smiled.

Although I did not know it then, control was already lost. As I say, some outcomes are unalterable.

That night, we made love, but it was different. It was no longer a test of virility, or another desperate biological exercise in the hope of conception. Now it was just the two of us again, after all this time, yearning for one another with an intense hunger that we fought to satisfy until, finally, we became one. How I had missed her. Afterwards, we lay in each other's arms, naked, silent, crying – not for our loss, I hoped, but rather for our elation at rediscovering each other. In reality, though, it was both of these things.

I awoke suddenly in the early hours, in mid-sentence.

I was kneeling on the bed, naked.

Before me, Caroline was also kneeling, staring at me in confusion.

Beside us, tall curtains flapped and swung in the breeze.

I squinted through the darkness.

'We were talking,' I whispered. 'What was I

saying? I was saying something. It was very, very important.'

'I don't know,' Caroline said shakily. 'What's going on, Charlie? I'm scared.'

'I suppose we were… sleep-talking. It's all right. Too much prosecco. Come here.'

Caroline trembled beneath my touch, but some time later we fell asleep again, and when I woke up bright sunlight was spilling across the marbled ceiling and floor.

Outside, a solemn bell tolled the hour and echoed about the streets of Verona.

****

After a light hotel breakfast, we ventured into the sunshine towards Piazza Brà, where pigeons swooped and settled in regular waves, and terracotta facades sat dwarfed by the gigantic structure of the amphitheatre. We did not speak of what had happened the previous night. Caroline seemed to have forgotten about it, which was almost as strange as the occurrence itself, but I didn't care. It was so refreshing to see the excited smile on her face again.

I had prepared an itinerary for both days, taking in the entire city, but had purposefully left it at the hotel. As she had said, it was time to relax now and let go of the controls.

By a small grassy oval, Caroline hopped on to the tourist train, which was a bright-yellow faux steam train with a trail of open carriages. Since we were the only passengers, the driver swiftly sold us our tickets before heading off into the city with a loud 'Toot toot'.

It was bumpy and fast, and Caroline giggled like a child as we jerked backwards and forwards through the beeping traffic, thumping over pavements and cobbles. But soon the driver found a clear path and, as we headed past the impressive brick structure of the old castle, Castelvecchio, and along the narrow street of Corso Cavour, a warm breeze stole off the

River Adige's emerald waters, filled with the heady scent of Verona.

Further along Corso Cavour, we stopped in traffic beside a crumbling archway.

Cast-iron gates partially blocked my view, but I saw the figure of a small boy standing motionless behind them: black hair against grey, withered skin; dark sockets where eyes should have been; mouth hanging agape in a terrible yawn.

I almost shouted in fear, yet somehow managed to control myself.

Despite the warmth, the fine hairs on my neck stood on end as I twisted away from his sightless gaze.

Caroline was smiling into the sunshine through bug-eye sunglasses. I was glad that she had not seen the child. When I turned to look again, he had gone.

The remainder of the train journey passed without incident. As we crossed the Adige and continued through the city and back towards Piazza Brà, I tried to convince myself that I had imagined the child, that he simply hadn't been there. But I could not: I knew what I had seen. It was impossible, but real. The boy had been dead. But then, I told myself as we disembarked and I followed Caroline through a maze of side streets in search of Juliet's balcony, it could have been a prank, a child in some kind of mask. Yes, surely that was the explanation. A trick.

Eventually, we found Casa di Giulietta and the ornate balcony above its paved square. As is often the case, finding the attraction was more interesting than the attraction itself and so we headed back into the streets to find somewhere to eat.

We backtracked, hoping to find a restaurant that we had passed just minutes earlier, but at some point, late in the morning, we found ourselves in an unfamiliar side street, where crimson ivy clung to high buildings on either side. All the blue and green shutters were closed. Except for the distant twittering of small birds, there was no sign of life.

'I think we're lost again,' I said.

'No,' Caroline replied, wandering further up the alley. 'I think it's this way.'

As we continued, a warm breeze rustled the leaves beside us. Dust swirled up from the pavement. There was something else too. I recognised the smell in the wind. We were near the river again.

My heart sank as we reached the end of the alleyway, because I realised that we were, once again, at Corso Cavour. The crumbling archway was directly opposite now, on the other side of the street.

This time, its gates were open.

Let's go in,' Caroline said. 'It's a church. Come on.'

As we crossed the road, I realised Caroline was right. The gold plaque on the wall beside the archway read: 'Chiesa di San Lorenzo'.

The archway opened on to a small courtyard with an ornamental well at its centre. Two cylindrical towers, constructed in bands of pale brick and pebbles, flanked the church's facade.

We walked through a darkened porch, into solemn coldness.

Before the altar, a group of tourists stood huddled around a small Italian guide who was explaining the history of the building. Although his accent was strong, his command of English was as polished as his shoes.

'San Lorenzo, as you see it now, was rebuilt at the beginning of the twelfth century. The massive earthquake of 1117 destroyed the previous church, which had stood since the fifth or sixth century. The rubble was used to reconstruct the towers as they are today. You will see the unique pattern of stone, brick and pebble around the towers.'

Sunlight streamed in from narrow, splayed windows, creating an orangey glow on the stone of the towers. I turned to Caroline, who was listening with interest.

'The plan is a Benedictine cross, divided into two areas by the transepts. You will see there are three naves, one large and then a smaller one to each side. Now, I will show you something very interesting.'

He walked beneath the supporting pillars that led to the south transept. His shining black shoes clicked and echoed in the silence as the tourists followed.

Caroline smiled mischievously as she let the group fall out of sight, before following quietly.

'Here we have the main window, with the stained glass. Broken glass from the earthquake was saved and the window was re-created as you see it now. In the central window, we have Jesus on the cross, and then beside him the saints are weeping. Now, at the bottom of the first window, here, you have a unicorn – a one-horned goat – resting his head on a woman's lap. This image has been used for many centuries in religion. It symbolises the incarnation of Jesus. The horn of the unicorn is the phallic symbol.

'But' – he turned to his audience with lifted finger – 'in all other windows around the world, the unicorn is white. This is the only church in the world that has a black unicorn on its glass. In the next picture there is a boy and then, in the next, we have the woman again. The child is gone and now she holds the death's head. The next picture is obscured, and we cannot see the end to our story. Now, if you will follow, time is running out and we must go to the next destination.'

Seconds later, Caroline and I were alone in the church. I went to the window to inspect the images more closely. The black unicorn, with the words BESTIA INCARNATA across its abdomen, had red, glaring eyes and razor teeth. In the next image, the boy was no more than a vague silhouette on the glass. Then the woman again, sitting once more, holding a pale skull – the death's head. Dark locks fell about her shoulders and there was the faintest impression of a smile on her lips. Something cold and nameless ran through me.

As the guide had said, the following picture at the base of the third window was scratched and worn beyond recognition. All that was left was the bright, tinted glass in the Veronese sunlight.

I jumped as Caroline spoke.

'Look at this, Charlie.'

I went to her. She was standing by a glass cabinet. Inside were two ancient ceremonial daggers on a stand.

Again, I felt it, just as I had done in Burley, at the Webbers' house, a sense that we were no longer alone, that someone stood behind us in the nave of the church. Caroline must have felt it too. She turned quickly and let out a sharp breath. But there was nothing. Only the silence, and the cold.

A cloud passed over the sun and the church fell into darkness around us.

'Let's get out of here,' she said. 'Please.'

Out in the courtyard, she recovered herself quickly.

'That was horrible,' she said, taking a long, deep breath. 'It felt like something terrible was about to happen.'

'Old churches can be like that. Look, the sun's coming out again. Let's find somewhere to eat. I'm starving.'

Caroline moved around the stone well and towards the church again. For a moment I thought she was going to go back inside, but she stopped short to stare at the exterior wall. I went over to join her.

Set over the brickwork, carved in granite, was a weather-worn coat of arms: a shield, encompassing the profile of a unicorn's head with two upturned daggers, one on each side.

As we left the courtyard and walked back down Corso Cavour, I noticed an old gypsy woman standing on the opposite side of the street, hunched over a stick and staring at us intently.

We had lunch at Caffè Rialto, beneath the vast limestone structure of Porta Borsari, the city's ancient Roman gate. We sat under a parasol, snacking on pistachios and fresh, warm bread dipped in virgin olive oil and vinegar. A half-carafe of white wine arrived and I poured us each a glass.

When I looked up at Caroline, I saw that she had removed her sunglasses and was staring at me with a solemn expression.

'Sarah told me something, when I stayed with her.'

'Sisters will talk,' I said, taking a sip of wine and smiling.

'I'm serious, Charlie.'

'OK, I'm listening.'

'She told me she can't have children either.'

This was a revelation to me. It seemed extraordinary that, during all the years that we had been trying for a baby, she had never told Caroline about it. Typical, I thought. Only Sarah could be that selfish. I felt the familiar resentment stir inside me. How could she?

'When did she find out?'

'Over two years ago.'

'So why didn't she tell you sooner? I don't get it. Weren't you angry? I mean, she could have supported you, shared your burden. It's unbelievable –'

'It's a very personal thing. People deal with it in

different ways and⋯ no,' she said quietly, and I could see tears welling in her eyes. 'I wasn't angry. That's the problem.'

I reached for her hand across the table.

'I was glad,' she continued, unable to meet my gaze. 'There, I've said it.'

'Caroline, there's no shame in that. It's totally understandable.'

'How?'

'Because now you don't have to live the rest of your life worrying about when your sister will conceive and give birth. Now you won't have to watch as she raises her own children. That's why. Because now you are not alone in all of this.'

'But it's wrong to be glad. Just wrong.'

'You feel sorry for her too, though, yes?'

'Of course.'

'Caroline, listen to me. You are human.'

'And you are kind.'

She smiled again and wiped tears from her eyes. Her eyeliner had smudged but it didn't matter. She looked incredible.

At that moment, Caroline screamed.

The old woman I had seen earlier was suddenly beside our table and had clutched Caroline's arm with a withered grip. Spit burst from her toothless mouth as she jabbered away in Italian. I understood nothing, although I heard the word once again – '*ragazzo*' – and also '*Galilei*'.

Her misty eyes were filled with madness. I stood up and grabbed her arm hard until she moaned in pain.

'Go away!' I shouted, and she cowered pathetically before me.

In her hand she held a string of rosary beads. She threw it feebly on to the table in front of Caroline, again making her cry out.

Waiters flocked around us and forced the old woman back out on to the street, shouting at her with upraised arms as she hobbled away.

We left shortly afterwards, abandoning the meal, and made our way back through the side streets. Caroline was visibly shaken. I held her hand and felt the rosary between us.

'She wanted me to have it,' she said.

Back at the hotel, she fell asleep immediately, as though drained of all energy. We had been in the sun for a long time, walked a fair way and drunk wine too. The final incident at Caffè Rialto had worn her out completely. I kissed her forehead and went back outside alone. There was something I needed to do.

****

Vicolo Listone was less intimidating by day and the Capra Nera was empty save for a few couples enjoying wine in the sun.

Stefano acknowledged me with his customary bow and smile.

'Welcome again, Mr Carter. You have lost your wife?'

'Almost,' I told him. 'But we're back on track now, thanks to you. I'll take a beer please, Stefano, in the shade there.'

As I waited, I stared up into the azure Italian sky. A tiny white aircraft slowly traversed the space, an unwelcome reminder that we had only one day left before it was time to fly home.

Stefano returned with a cold beer and I sipped at it slowly until the last of the customers were gone.

'You would like something else?'

'There is one thing you can help with. "Stanza del Ragazzo Tranquillo,"' I said. 'What does it mean?'

A curious look crossed his bronzed face. The beaming smile faltered momentarily before he answered.

'You are staying at Hotel Galilei then, yes?'

I nodded.

'Wait. I will bring another drink and sit with you, if it is OK?'

He returned with a glass of wine for himself and a small beer, which he placed before me. Once seated, he brushed black locks from his face and lit a cigarette.

'Stanza del Ragazzo Tranquillo.' He nodded. 'The Room of the Quiet Boy.'

I thought of the boy I had seen behind the gates of the San Lorenzo church. I remembered the dark holes where his eyes should have been. I thought of Mrs Webber and the terrified look on her face when she had mouthed the word '*ragazzo*'.

'The room has this name because of what happen at the hotel, maybe twenty years ago, more I think, all before I work here.' He took a sip of wine and nodded at a staff member before continuing.

'A young couple come to Verona, from England, like you and your wife. They also bring their child. A small boy, six years old perhaps, no more. They stay at the hotel. Everything is good — they enjoy the city, they explore, they eat, drink — but then, on the third night, in the middle of the night, something happen. The boy, he disappears. Gone in the dark. Everybody search: the police, the hotel staff, the people of Verona. They even search the river. Nothing. He is vanished. Very sad. They never find him, even now.'

Stefano pulled on his cigarette and blew smoke into the light.

'Some people,' he said, 'they think the couple kill their son. Some people think he is walking in his sleep and fell into the river – drowned. Me? I do not know. How can I know? All I know is the boy is never found and the couple, they go back to England, alone.'

'That's terrible,' I said.

Stefano nodded and stubbed out his cigarette. He stared at me with dark, serious eyes.

'They say the boy does not rest. That his essence, it stays here, in this world, here in Verona, in Hotel Galilei. You understand?'

We turned in early that night. I was exhausted. The travelling and the initial elation on arriving in Verona, not to mention the wine and beer, had caught up with me. I mentioned nothing of my conversation with Stefano. Why would I? It would only have spoilt things if Caroline had known that we were sleeping in the very same room from which a child had disappeared, all those years ago.

Caroline fell straight to sleep but I had trouble dropping off. I could hear the occupants of the next suite chatting in deep Italian tones.

I watched Caroline sleeping. She was so childlike in that peaceful state, gently breathing in and out. In her hand she still held the rosary, its silver crucifix glinting in the moonlight.

Eventually, I fell into a deep and dreamless sleep until I awoke suddenly in the middle of the night, certain that a loud noise had stirred me. But when I listened there was nothing, only Caroline's even breaths cutting through the silence.

When I woke again, sunbeams were playing over the marble ceiling. The windows were open and Caroline was in the shower, singing with abandon. I got up and joined her.

We spent the morning exploring the amphitheatre, wandering around its dark, labyrinthine underbelly and then up on to its crumbling stands. Blinding sunlight spilt across the oval interior, and from the arena's crown Piazza Brà was a toy set. Miniature cars and people wove in and out of the city's alleyways.

We ate pizza by the river, then ventured out again later to shop along Via Mazzini, where the window displays carried no price tags and the shop interiors were decorated in polished marble. I bought Caroline a new white shirt and a pair of sunglasses for her growing collection. She beamed with happiness.

Later, as shadows lengthened over the cobbles, we took a side alley to make our way back.

There were no shops here, only decrepit facades with tightly closed shutters and decaying wooden doors. Small gargoyles, crouching on rooftops, glared at us as we turned down another narrow lane.

Caroline gasped.

A beggar woman stood before us. Dirty and draped in black, she cradled a baby in one arm and pleaded in Italian, holding out a shaking palm. I put her in her early thirties, but it was difficult to tell. She was thin and looked crazed with hunger. I glanced back down the alley to make sure it wasn't a trap. Nobody was there.

When I turned back, I saw that Caroline was stroking the child's black hair with a smile. She gave the woman some lira from her jeans pocket.

'*Grazie.*' The woman nodded in appreciation. '*Grazie, grazie.*'

Caroline reached into back her handbag, pulled out the rosary beads and placed them in the beggar's trembling hand.

'Good luck,' she whispered.

Back in the hotel room, I asked why she had given them away.

'She needs God's help more than we do.'

How little we knew.

Once again, I found it difficult to sleep. The guests in the room above were noisy, creaking over the floorboards, this way and that. At one point a great thud sounded, as though someone had dropped something heavy. Then all was quiet again.

I woke up in the early hours to find Caroline clinging to me tightly.

'There's someone here,' she whispered. 'In the room.'

I listened intently.

No noise came from the road outside, nor from anywhere within the hotel. There was no wind against the curtains; only the moonlight, streaming across the room and reflecting in the stained-glass partition.

The silence was absolute.

Then I felt it, or rather became suddenly aware of it. The knowledge that Caroline was right, that we were not alone, that something was here with us. The silence was unbearable as we clung to each other, a thickening silence filled with growing menace that made breathing almost impossible. But no, not menace, that is too weak a word. We were in the presence of an evil so pure that I felt my heart might explode inside my chest.

A shuffling sounded behind the partition, in the living area of the suite.

Caroline took a sharp intake of breath.

Had I seen movement behind the screen? Yes, I think so.

'It's there,' Caroline whispered. 'In the corner.'

I squinted through the gloom, to the living area

beyond the glass. To the corner, where shadows turned to blackness. There stood a shape which did not belong. A small outline of darkness; a pale, distorted face through the coloured glass.

'I can't breathe,' Caroline said. 'Please.'

I bolted out of bed, ran to the door, and switched the light on.

There was nothing in the corner. The silence was gone. A small breeze pushed at the curtains.

Caroline took a deep breath and started crying.

Whatever had been there, in the corner of our room, was now gone, but our fear remained. We sat huddled against the headboard for many minutes, trembling in each other's arms like frightened children.

We left the lights on and eventually lay down.

I held Caroline until the morning. I must have slept at some point, although I do not believe that she did.

****

Since we were scheduled to fly at 11am, we rose early, showered and had a light breakfast at the hotel. Afterwards, I told Caroline to wait for me in the cafe across the street while I brought down our bags and checked out. It is worthy of mockery but, even though the sky was overcast that morning, I have never been so glad of the daylight.

Neither Caroline nor I had ever been religious, although we always respected the beliefs of others and if we entered a holy place we would treat it with the reverence it deserved. I did not believe in ghosts, or that the dead could walk among the living. I had never seen a vision or heard a noise that would either prove or disprove the existence of ghosts, until now. And even now, with all that had happened in the room the previous night, I still held on to the fact that it could somehow be explained rationally, that either a trick had been played or a mistake of some kind made.

'We could have imagined it,' I said, as we waited for the cab to arrive. 'Last night.'

Caroline attempted to smile at my weak effort to convince her, but I could see the fear creeping back over her. She sipped at her espresso with a shaking hand.

'I should never have given the rosary away.

Please let's not talk about it anymore.'

I was having trouble coming to terms with any of this, and I was disappointed that our trip had been marred by the event, but I couldn't help seeing her logic.

On the first night, we had awoken, kneeling, facing each other, talking in our sleep. Then, during the first day, I had seen the boy behind the gates of San Lorenzo. Then later, in the church, we had both sensed a presence but, once the old woman had given Caroline the rosary, nothing else had occurred, until last night.

At Villafranca airport, I left Caroline in the executive lounge and made for the shops, where I purchased a new rosary, complete with mahogany beads and a solid silver crucifix.

'I love you,' she said as I gave it to her. 'Thank you for everything.'

How naive I was, to assume that a simple rosary would change anything. As I said, Father, sometimes God is not enough.

Before we boarded, we spent a little time sitting quietly in the modern airport chapel. I lit candles for my departed parents and Caroline did the same. Then she lit one more and placed it apart from the others, where it burned in the dimness on its own. When I asked her for whom it was intended, she would not say.

Sitting there in the chapel and holding Caroline's hand in the flickering light, I was overcome by a wave of sympathy. How difficult for her, to know we would never have our own children, and to return to England and continue teaching once again.

Later, on the plane, she became sleepy. I kissed her warm cheek.

'It means "Room of the Quiet Boy,"' she said, with closed eyes.

'I know. Stefano told me a boy went missing there, years ago.'

'He didn't go missing,' she whispered, as she drifted to sleep. 'He was murdered.'

****

In stark contrast to Hotel Galilei, Creech Lane Cottage was a chaos of unpacked boxes from the move and half-completed renovations, courtesy of the Hawthorns. Still, despite the mess and the blustery conditions, it was good to be home among the rolling Purbeck hills.

Nothing untoward occurred during those first weeks. I returned to work and secured a horde of new clients, bringing welcome revenue for Elliot Thorpe Financial. To my surprise, Caroline went back to her teaching with renewed enthusiasm. She seemed more relaxed, now that we had certainty in regard to our infertility. A door had closed and in its place a new, brighter one had opened. Where before she had been depressed and quiet, now she was upbeat and positive. Only occasionally would I recognise that sad longing, that distant faraway look in her green eyes that I had known so well before.

I understand it better now. It is in the nature of evil to fashion a counterfeit security, to bide its time in a landscape of normality until finally, when least expected, it can rise up and fold its dark wings about the light.

I say that nothing untoward occurred, but there was something: the nightmares. Always the same.

I found myself in Verona, wandering through

abandoned streets at nightfall, lost in deserted, ancient alleyways until finally, once again, I stood in Corso Cavour, before the crumbling archway of San Lorenzo.

The two cylindrical towers loomed overhead as I entered the church. My footsteps broke the silence and echoed about the stony pillars and vaulted ceilings. I crossed the nave to the window in the south transept.

Moonlight illuminated the stained glass: the black unicorn with red, glaring eyes, resting his head on the woman's lap; the vague silhouette of the boy, and then the woman again, holding a pale skull in her hand with the faintest suggestion of a smile on her lips. And then what? What was the next picture? I could almost see it through the faded, scratched glass: the boy again, was it? Or was it something else? Dread crept over me.

I looked down to find my hands covered with fresh, crimson blood.

I awoke screaming on each occasion, drenched with sweat, and with Caroline beside me, stroking my hair and telling me it was just a dream.

For the most part, we concentrated our spare time on the cottage, clearing the place in readiness for redecoration.

In an attempt to modernise the interior, the

Hawthorns had boarded and skimmed an entire wall in the dining room. The finish was rough and unpainted, and I spent many evenings sanding and layering white emulsion across its surface until it was perfect again. It was strange but satisfying to be completing all that the Hawthorns had begun. The other rooms were not so simple. The ceramic in the upstairs bathroom, though solid enough, was worn and stained beyond repair. Tiles had cracked and in places fallen away completely, leaving a mess of crumbling adhesive and rough grouting in their absence.

The garden also required attention. The dry stone walls around the perimeter had collapsed in places, the roses needed pruning, and the lawns to the front and back were riddled with wild flowers and weeds. So we made time in the evenings, now that the sun was setting later, to attend to these things together. It was good to spend time together again.

When we spoke of Verona, it was of sunshine, romance, the amphitheatre, the exquisite food at the Capra Nera. We never mentioned San Lorenzo, or what we had experienced in our hotel room. It was odd, but I knew that, if I broached the subject with Caroline, she would have stopped me; and also that, if the tables were turned, I would have done the same. Perhaps we were frightened of mentioning it lest, in doing so, we should conjure the darkness once again. Perhaps we wanted to forget. If only life were so simple. In the end, though, I knew it was never far from Caroline's mind. She carried with her everywhere the rosary I had bought at Villafranca.

'Let's go for a walk,' she said, one evening in June. 'It's beautiful outside. We could go to Tyneham.'

I sometimes wonder whether, had I simply said no that day, we could have avoided having to endure everything that was to follow; whether it simply would not have happened. But this is ridiculous, of course. You cannot alter the path of fate. You cannot change destiny. It is as permanent and unyielding as the jagged cliffs at Tyneham, and as relentless and foreboding as the dark, rolling ocean beneath.

Ten minutes later, having parked on the sloping field above the village, we walked amid the ruins of the forgotten village. At this time in the evening we were the only visitors.

Being the parish priest of the village's only intact building, St Mary's, you will know, Father, that Churchill's war cabinet deemed the land necessary for D-Day preparations, and that the villagers were summarily evicted and never permitted to return. The evacuation was decreed in the winter of 1943. The Ministry of Defence controls the land to this day. But that is only the modern history, for the place is mentioned in the Domesday Book of 1086, and even before that there is evidence of an earlier settlement, a Roman occupation dating from the invasion of Britain, shortly after the death of Christ.

'It's so sad here,' Caroline whispered, as though she might stir the dead, as we wandered through the main thoroughfare. 'All of those poor people, losing their homes. Never coming back.'

The skeletal structures, toothed and roofless, each with empty doorways and blank, frameless windows, were solemn and beautiful against the overgrown setting. A thick carpet of ferns obscured many interiors but here and there long-forgotten fireplaces, crumbling and blackened, could be glimpsed on ivy-clad walls. The sun was bright but low, and our shadows stretched before us like giant insects as we passed a small pond where dragonflies hovered and darted over water lilies. In the great oaks above, the twittering of small birds filled the silence. A light breeze stirred, scented with sea salt and wild lavender, as we turned and made our way back through the village.

Caroline walked on ahead.

'This way.'

Beyond the car park, we crossed a small bridge. A flowing stream sounded in the darkness far below.

We turned on to a wide, chalky path that I knew led to the cliffs at Worbarrow. A steep incline rose to our left where a herd of sheep grazed on unkempt grass. Beside us, a wooded corridor, thick with undergrowth and gloomy shadows, stretched the length of the path as far as the eye could see.

We had walked for only a few minutes when I noticed that the birds had ceased their evening song. The only sound now was the distant gushing of water from the woodland, where the stream must have been. The wind had died to nothing. I felt Caroline's hand tighten in mine as we continued.

A sudden thumping sound drew my attention to the hillside, where the sheep now charged in unison to its crest before disappearing over the grassy barrow.

There was something else too. The fresh sea air had gone and in its place a foul, rotting stench that I instantly associated with decay and old death filled the atmosphere.

We were being watched by someone, or something. Of that I was certain. Instinctively, I turned to the path we had walked. Nothing. Only the empty trail, leading back to the bridge. The stillness.

Caroline's grip tensed around my hand in a vice-like hold. Her emerald eyes were transfixed by the woodland and the blood had drained from her face.

Her expression of fear sent a terrible shudder through me.

I followed her gaze into the trees, into the dark undergrowth, to a willow tree in the tangled weeds. Its green tendrils swayed slightly, although there was no breeze. What had unsettled its branches? An animal?

A dark shape stirred behind the curtain of dangling branches. I squinted into the darkness. Yes, someone was in there, behind the greenery, in the shadow of the willow.

Caroline moaned in terror as the boy slid into sight. He wore a dark suit, and his hair, blacker than night, was neatly brushed to one side. There was no doubt in my mind that it was the same child I had seen in Verona, behind the gates of San Lorenzo. Shadows played about the woodland, making it hard to discern his features, but the two gaping holes where his eyes should have been were impossible to deny. The pallor of his skin was grey and shrivelled, but somehow waxen too. A dreadful malevolence filled the atmosphere. An indescribable menace. Was he smiling?

Caroline took a step forward and then collapsed into my arms. She had fainted.

I caught Caroline's fall, easing her gently on to the

chalky path and resting her head on my thigh. She was out cold for some moments. Occasionally her body twitched and hardened like stone before falling limp again. I willed myself to remain calm, in control, not to glance towards the trees, the willow, where even now I felt the boy's sightless stare emanating from the shadows.

Eventually, as she lay with me, the birds resumed their twittering, the warm breeze returned and the air became light once more. I could smell the sea again. Trusting in the palpable change of atmosphere, I steeled myself to look back. There was nothing now, only the trees, gently swaying and rustling. The boy was gone.

Caroline came around and I helped her to her feet. She trembled and staggered like a drunk, so I lifted and carried her the short distance to the car, where I helped her into the passenger seat.

On the drive back home, she remained silent. I thought she might have fainted again, but when I looked she was staring across the passing fields with tears in her eyes.

I was badly shaken as well, and the moment we returned home I poured a shot of whisky and drank it down in one gulp.

'Drink this,' I said, offering her one. 'It'll take the edge off.'

'I knew it would follow us,' she said, as she cupped the tumbler in her shaking hands. 'I knew the moment we left Verona it wasn't over. That was the start, Charlie. Don't you see?'

'Come on. Drink up.'

'You can't pretend it's not happening.'

'It could have been a trick of the light,' I said, but it sounded unconvincing, even to me. 'Or a prank of some kind.'

'What kind of prank or trick could possibly –'

She stopped herself in mid-sentence, looking around the kitchen nervously. I had felt it too, a sudden drop in temperature. A thickening, hateful silence growing as the seconds passed, accompanied by a chilling awareness that we were no longer alone.

'I don't think we should talk about it any more tonight.'

'Agreed.'

Soon afterwards, the tension lifted. Normality returned to the cottage.

Caroline went to bed and asked me not to be too long. She was frightened and I didn't blame her. So was I, Father, for I knew there had been no trick of the light or bizarre prank. We had seen the dead boy, the same *ragazzo* Mrs Webber had spoken of all those weeks ago, the same apparition I had witnessed in Verona and that we had sensed in our hotel room. Something was happening and it was beyond our control or comprehension. All we had was each other and the hope that nothing else would happen. But already, for Caroline at least, that hope had slipped away. As she had said, Verona had been just the beginning.

I was awoken by a loud noise in the night. I could still hear it ringing in the silence as I sat bolt upright in bed. I listened hard. I was certain the noise had come from downstairs.

Thud.

There it was again, louder this time, echoing about the kitchen below.

Thud. Thud. Thud.

I leapt up and switched on the light, realising in that moment that Caroline was no longer lying beside me.

Thud. Thud. Thud. Thud.

'Caroline,' I shouted. 'Where are you?'

On it went, reverberating through the cottage as I lurched down the stairs and into the kitchen.

I found nothing and so charged on through the living room, calling out as I went, but then I stopped dead as I reached the cold silence of the dining room.

Caroline stood, dressed in her pale night gown, facing the centre of the northern wall. The wall I had spent so much time layering with emulsion paint.

For a moment she was utterly motionless.

Blood was smeared across the wall's white surface, so much blood.

Then she raised her hand and I saw the kitchen knife glint for a moment in the moonlight as she buried it deep in the wall, again and again – *thud, thud* – each time tearing a dark gash in the plasterboard and casting spatters of crimson on to the surrounding wall.

'Caroline!'

She carried on as though unaware of my presence, stabbing and stabbing at the wall, each time more deeply than the last.

Quietly, I crossed the room and gently rested my hands on her shoulders.

She became still once again.

Her hands dropped slowly to her sides. I turned her to face me and took the knife from her clenched fist.

Her gaze was blank and void of emotion. Flecks of deep red blood speckled her pale skin. Her breaths were quiet and calm and even.

She was sleepwalking.

I put down the knife and led her by the hand, away from the wall. She glided beside me in silence as we left the dining room and entered the living room. Once I had seated her in an armchair, I switched on a side lamp to get a closer look at her wounds.

The lacerations, on her forefinger and right hand palm, were too shallow to require stitching, but deep and clean enough to continue seeping with blood. I rested her palms upwards on the knees of her gown, before finding the first-aid kit and cleaning and dressing the cuts as best I could.

All the while, Caroline remained silent, breathing quietly and gazing vacantly into space. When I was finished, I led her upstairs to bed and, after making sure that she was comfortable and asleep with her eyes shut, I returned to the dining room and switched on the spotlights.

The extent of the damage was clear in the orangey glow. Caroline had targeted a particular area, halfway up the wall, which was now riddled with holes and smeared with blood. I ran my fingers over its irregular surface and a small clump of plasterboard fell away into the darkness inside.

In an attempt to remove the damaged area, I pencilled out a square around the bloodied abrasions and then used a Stanley knife to cut it out. The new blade cut easily through the thin layers of board, and when I was done I used a palette knife to lever the jagged square from its frame.

As I moved away, the spotlight picked out ancient stone beneath.

I do not know how long I stood there, Father, staring into the dimness. It seemed like an eternity. Every muscle, every sinew in my body was taut with fear. The room had grown cold around me. My heart thumped like a wild animal against my ribcage.

It was impossible, but what faced me, in the darkness beyond the makeshift wall that the Hawthorns had erected, was the original cottage wall and, on it, raised from the brickwork, was a coat of arms, carved in intricate stone: a unicorn, flanked by two upturned daggers.

I filled a mug with neat whisky and sat trembling in a chair beside Caroline as she slept. I left the light on for fear of what might happen in the dark.

My mind was alive and racing with questions and theories and impossibilities. I tried to apply logic, to understand rationally how such a coincidence could occur, but it was useless. In the end, gulping down whisky and watching Caroline breathing steadily before me, I was gripped by an unspeakable sense of dread: a feeling that we no longer controlled events, that every decision we made, or had made, had somehow been predestined, and that now we were being led, or rather had been led, all the way to Verona, to the church of San Lorenzo. But worse still, that something terrible had returned with us.

At some point I fell asleep in the chair. My dreams were plagued by lurid, stained-glass images that shifted and melted into one another like a kaleidoscope of dark horrors: a black unicorn with eyes of fire, writhing, twisting, turning before finally becoming a child with hollow sockets for eyes. Then the pale-faced woman, etched into leaded glass, holding the skull, the death's head, smiling gently all the while. Then another image – far more harrowing – but as I awoke, screaming, it left my consciousness, out of reach, and I made no further attempt to recall it.

****

The following morning I was twitchy and exhausted. I was due in Bournemouth early for a directors' meeting and knew that heavy traffic would delay my journey. It was Hugo's mid-year summary of our current financial position and future plans, an important gathering from which my absence would not be forgiven. All the same, I explained to Caroline as best I could the events of the previous night, and then showed her what lay behind the dining-room wall.

For the longest time, she said nothing as she gazed at the stony coat of arms, her face ashen with a mixture of fear and disbelief.

'It's not possible,' she said vacantly. 'How can it be possible?'

I tried to reassure her, telling her there must be a reasonable explanation, but it was no use.

'It's all been planned somehow, from the beginning.'

I shuddered as I remembered asking her where she had wanted to go, all those weeks ago, and the way her voice had sounded, like a child's, when she had spoken the word 'Verona'.

'Charlie, we have to get out of here. We have to leave.'

'Just stay calm, I said. 'We'll work this out. Just

stay here until I come home and don't do anything. I'll be back as quick as I can. Please.'

Although I was concerned for Caroline's wellbeing, I will admit that being at work that morning was strangely therapeutic, the sense of clear structure and normality deeply comforting. Even Hugo's voice, droning into the silence of the boardroom as he outlined plans for further expansion, was reassuring. Even the polished, walnut table around which we sat, with symmetrical, butterfly-like patterns across its surface, was somehow solid and secure, without ambiguity or riddle.

'What's wrong, Charles?' Hugo asked suspiciously, once the other directors had left the room. 'You've barely said a word all morning. You're shaking like an old dog and you look awful. You haven't even shaved.'

'I feel terrible,' I admitted. 'The truth is, I've barely slept, I was so ill last night. I'm sorry, but would you mind if I go home once I've completed my paperwork?'

Hugo nodded from behind steepled fingers, examining me with concern.

'Everything all right on the home front?'

What was I to tell him? That we were being haunted? That I had seen ghosts and felt the presence of evil, both here and in Verona? That the world we had once understood was now a confusion of past and present, of the living and the dead?

'Everything's fine.'

Minutes later, I stood before the mirror in the toilet with my hands in front of me. Hugo was right. I was shaking and dark rings circled my eyes. My skin was pale and unshaven. I splashed water on my face and spat into the sink, almost retching. What was happening to me? What was happening to us?

I returned early in the afternoon to find Creech Lane Cottage empty. Caroline's car was gone and I would have panicked, had it not been for the note she had left on the kitchen table:

Charlie, don't worry about me. Back at five x

I took the opportunity to get some rest upstairs, but my senses were heightened and tuned even in sleep for I awoke to the sound of Caroline's car on the driveway and went straight outside to meet her.

As I approached, she wound down the window.

'Get in,' she said. 'I need to speak with you, but not here.'

She drove us out through the hills, away from the coast towards Wareham, before turning off into a heavily forested area. The light was dim here, even in bright sunlight, and I knew exactly where she was heading. I noticed she wore plasters on her hands now, in place of the bandages I had put on.

We parked in the shade of the Silent Lady Inn and found a table in the upper gardens, secluded from the main seating areas. Evening sunlight slanted across the grass and all was silent except for the occasional seagull, screeching overhead.

'I didn't want to talk at the cottage,' she said, as I returned to the table with our drinks. 'I was worried that –'

'You don't need to explain. I completely understand.'

'No,' she said. 'You don't.'

'What do you mean?'

'I found some things out today, Charlie, about the cottage. Or rather, about the previous owners.'

'The Hawthorns?'

'No, a long time before them. Twenty years or more. I went to see Emerson Briars today. The older estate agent told me the cottage had been empty for two decades before the Hawthorns moved in. They'd been trying to sell it for years. He remembers the previous owners from his early days on the job. Harold and Elizabeth Knight. They had a six-year-old. A boy called Tom. They took a trip to Italy, to Verona, and returned without the boy. They said he'd been lost, disappeared or taken. The police were involved – even sent to Italy – but to no avail. The couple were devastated. Their bodies were found at Creech Lane Cottage. Suicide.'

'Jesus.'

'I know, that wasn't in the particulars, was it? But don't you see? It's the Knights. They're the key to it all.'

'Yes,' I said, 'I do see that. But I don't understand why.'

A silence fell between us and Caroline caught me with a nervous stare. She sighed loudly and took a large sip of wine before continuing. Somewhere in the trees nearby, a crow cawed and flapped about before becoming silent again.

'I lied to you,' she said. 'In Verona.'

'What do you mean?'

'That first night at the hotel. We woke in the middle of the night, facing each other. We'd been sleep-talking, remember?'

'Yes,' I replied. 'I was saying something and I couldn't remember what it was. And you said –'

'That I couldn't remember either,' she broke in. 'But I lied. I woke up before you. I heard exactly what you said. You were talking about someone called Tom, but your voice sounded as though it belonged to someone else. It wasn't your voice at all, it was deeper.'

She rubbed at her temples and looked away, as

though deciding whether or not to continue. I wasn't sure whether I wanted to hear what she had to say either.

'You said you murdered him in the bathroom.' She gulped at the memory. 'You said that you⋯ strangled him until he was dead, but that his eyes still watched you, and that you gouged them out with a knife but it made no difference. That he still stared. You wrapped him up in a blanket and covered his head, then carried him down to the church in the middle of the night. There was an old well there and you threw him down, into the darkness. You heard water at the bottom, but you said it was running water, that you knew it would all end up in the river. You said⋯ you said the whole thing had been a success and now we just needed to convince everyone that Tom had wandered off in the night. We just needed to get home. Then you woke up.'

I shuddered as I remembered what Caroline had said on the plane before falling asleep – that the boy had been murdered, not lost. Now I understood the certainty that I had heard in her voice. I glanced uneasily around the clearing in which we were sitting. No one was there. To anyone watching, we would simply look like a couple enjoying a drink in the sunshine. No one could possibly guess at the horrors that we were discussing.

'Why didn't you tell me? You should have said something.'

'I didn't want to ruin the holiday, so in the morning I just pretended the whole thing had never happened, that I'd heard nothing.'

'No one would do that to their own son. It's evil.'

'But you know that he did. You've seen him. He has no eyes.'

I remembered her lighting the extra candle at the airport and shivered again.

'I still don't understand what this has to do with us. Why is this happening?'

Caroline nodded seriously. She had obviously given this consideration already.

'I believe the Knights are still at Creech Lane Cottage,' she said quietly. 'I believe that they murdered their child in Verona and that they do not rest in death. When we bought the house everything was fine, but I think our sadness in not being able to have children allowed them to reawaken, in us.'

'How do you mean?'

'I'm saying that, somehow, they got inside us. Our sadness allowed them in. They led us to Verona, to the hotel, even to the very room where it all happened, and to the church. Mr Knight spoke through you that night, as if he were re-enacting the events. When the boy comes, he is angry. He cannot rest either.'

I thought about it all for a moment. Caroline's reasoning made sense. Her voice had been different too, when she had spoken the word 'Verona'. Had she not sounded like a child, whispering? She had chosen the hotel. Even the first suite we had been offered had been unsuitable. It had to be that city, Verona; that hotel, Galilei; that room, Stanza del Ragazzo Tranquillo; and that church, San Lorenzo. Yes, we had been led.

'You have to be right,' I agreed. 'But how about this? What if the boy returned with us because he wanted us, you and me, to confirm to each other exactly what had happened to him, and how? Maybe he will rest now, knowing that we have said all this today and brought it out into the open.'

Caroline smiled weakly and I realised that I was two steps behind her. It was, of course, the reason why she had told me all she knew.

'I think we should sell up and leave,' she said. 'Just get out and never look back. I'm not sure what will happen if we stay.'

A silence fell between us.

'OK,' I replied, looking down at the blood-stained plasters on her hands. 'But let's just wait and see, just for a while. It may be settled already. I will pray that it is and you should do the same.'

Working at Elliot Thorpe over the following days was truly exhausting. A sudden dip in the markets brought a flood tide of investors looking for quick access to stocks and buying at what they considered to be a low price. Inundated with new enquiries, I struggled to keep pace and push transactions through before the markets lifted once again. As always, the less experienced investors were getting edgy and needed constant reassurance until the inevitable upturn began. Pulled in both directions, I fought to retain existing clients while appearing calm, collected and competent to the new ones. In reality though, the cracks were starting to show.

In every quiet moment, I was haunted by what the Knights had done to their son in Verona, and how their lifeless bodies had been found in the cottage all those years ago. How terrible it was: filicide and, finally, suicide. My nightmares could not be subdued either, even with whisky. I came to dread sleep but knew it was necessary to survive work.

At one point, Hugo asked me to ring the Webbers and make sure they were comfortable with the new trust arrangements but I could not bring myself to pick up the phone and speak with the woman who had foreseen all that was to come. To do so would be to tempt fate again, surely. Instead, I told Hugo I had done it and that all was well, hoping he would never find out.

On and on it went: just as I thought the markets had stabilised, there was another drop, a new raft of investors and more comforting phone calls to existing clients. We simply didn't have the staff to cope with the levels of new transactions, and I was sometimes leaving before dawn and not returning from home visits until well after nine in the evening. Even the weekends were spent catching up on paperwork. I barely saw Caroline during that period. She was usually asleep by the time I came home, and in the mornings I was gone before she had even stirred.

Towards the end of June, though, even through my punishing schedule, I saw changes in her. At first they were subtle, almost imperceptible: a fleeting, troubled look in her eyes or a quick, nervous biting of fingernails. But as the days passed, she began to lose colour. Her eyes, normally bright with energy, were now dulled and a haunted expression clung to her face, as though some inner battle were being fought, and lost, and she could not share any of it with me, or even let me help her in the fight.

'What's the matter,' I asked, one morning before I left for Bournemouth. 'Talk to me. Listen, I know I've been snowed under but what we talked about in the pub, I haven't forgotten. If you want to leave this place and sell up, then just say the word. All I want is to see you happy. You're so distant. I want us to be close again, like in Verona.'

'It wouldn't make any difference,' she replied, and I could see her love for me, shining through watery green eyes. 'It's too late.'

'What do you mean? Please talk to me. I love you.'

'I love you too, Charles Carter.'

'Tell me what you mean, it's too late?'

'I will talk to you, but I'm not quite there yet. Give me a little space. I promise I will when I'm ready.'

She had been this way before we had flown to Verona, and I wondered if her sadness had returned.

On the Thursday of the same week, I escaped from Elliot Thorpe by creating a couple of fictitious client meetings in my diary that meant I could not possibly return to Bournemouth that day. Before I left I received a message that Hugo wanted to see me but I ignored it because I could continue no longer. I was shaking and my head was throbbing from the pressure.

I arrived at Wareham primary school shortly before one o'clock and parked around the back, hoping to surprise Caroline and take her out for lunch somewhere special. I couldn't see her car in among the others, but decided she must have parked elsewhere that day.

I was buzzed into the main entrance and was immediately faced by an inquisitive stare from the ageing receptionist sitting behind her desk. It was the first time I had entered the school. A smell of disinfectant and old furniture polish hung in the air.

'I'm after Caroline Carter, please,' I said, looking around at the green walls, which were adorned with colourful children's paintings. 'I'm Charles, her husband.'

For a moment she was silent, observing me with a mixture of confusion and pity. Outside, children laughed and screamed in the sunshine.

'I'm very sorry, Mr Carter,' she replied, 'But Mrs Carter hasn't been at work for over a week now. She's ill at the moment.'

Twenty minutes later, as I passed Creech Lane Cottage, I spotted Caroline's green Fiat in the driveway. I drove on a little way, before parking on a grassy verge and making my way back towards the house on foot. I wanted to surprise her but, more than that, I wanted to know what she was doing.

My mind was racing with different scenarios as I crept over a collapsed section of the garden wall and approached the back door. What had she said? That it was 'too late'? Too late for what? For us? Was she having an affair? Yes, that must be it. Surely it would explain why she had been so distant and unable to discuss with me what was on her mind. She was consumed with guilt. But who was he? A fellow teacher? A parent of one of the children?

I opened the back door silently and stole through to the kitchen.

Caroline screamed with fright as I entered the room to find her sitting at the kitchen table with an array of papers spread out before her.

'Charles, what are you –'

'No,' I broke in, evenly. 'What are *you* doing? What have *you* been doing for the past week?'

A thick silence filled the space between us. Caroline looked up at me vacantly, then down at the papers around her. One was a photocopy, a line drawing of a small chapel. I didn't recognise the place, but I knew the architecture well enough. Two cylindrical towers, flanking its entrance: an exact replica of San Lorenzo, only smaller and set among surrounding hills, with a dark ocean in the background.

'I was wrong,' she said finally. 'Wrong about everything.'

'What are you talking about?'

'Emerson Briars lied to us. Mr Hawthorn was never made redundant. He quit his job after his wife committed suicide. She was found hanging at Tyneham, in the woods. He never went back to work. That's why the bank repossessed the house. He just··· gave up on everything. They say he went mad.'

Her voice was distant and unemotional as she continued. She did not meet my eye.

'Julie Hawthorn had been unable to cope with the death of her baby boy. It was recorded as a cot death. It happened here, in this house. She was buried at the graveyard at Tyneham, next to the child, Samuel. He was six months old. Not long after the funeral, the vicar noticed something wrong with the graves. The soil had been tampered with. Police were called in. The bodies were gone. They tried to find Mr Hawthorn, but he'd disappeared too. Three days later his body was found washed up on a beach at Eastbourne, just near Beachy Head. It's a popular suicide spot. Always has been, apparently. The cliffs are five hundred feet high there. There's little chance of surviving from that height. No one ever has.

'At first I thought it could be a coincidence, the Hawthorns and the Knights – both losing a child, being unable to cope – but I know now. It was no cot death. She killed *her* son, too. There can be no mistaking.'

I approached the kitchen table slowly. I could see that Caroline was on the edge of something. I drew up a chair quietly and sat down opposite her.

'A year earlier, the Hawthorns had taken a holiday,' she continued. 'Verona. I checked with the hotel, told them I was a relative. They stayed at Hotel Galilei too. I've been talking to the vicar at Tyneham. Nice chap. Young. He hasn't been there long. He's called Father Henry. Did you know that in the past fifty years a grave at Tyneham has only ever been tampered with once before? And guess whose grave it was. Elizabeth Knight's. Her body was exhumed and stolen as well.'

A sinking feeling settled over me as a tear welled up in Caroline's eye. I sensed the worst was yet to come.

'I did some other research, Charlie, at the parish records in Wareham. Marriages, births, deaths. Julie Hawthorn and Elizabeth Knight had something else in common. They shared the same maiden name. You know what it was? Timpson.'

'Please stop it, Caroline,' I whispered. 'That's impossible.'

The temperature in the room dropped significantly at that moment. A watchful, dominating silence filled the air around us. I just wanted her to be quiet. I simply did not want to know why Elizabeth

Knight and Julie Hawthorn had the same maiden name as my own wife.

'Impossible but true. I was led, Charlie, led to Italy. He wanted to show me, make me understand where it all began. It came from Verona. At first I thought Harold Knight was a monster; now I know he was the only man ever to help.'

'What do you mean? Look, there has to be a rational explanation for –'

'There's another chapel at Tyneham,' she continued, as though not hearing me. 'It's just a ruin now. You'd never know it was there. It was destroyed in 1623. There was an earth tremor of some kind. It looked like this once. Familiar isn't it? Italian architecture, wouldn't you say?'

She me passed me the photocopy of the line drawing.

'In 1620, three years before it was destroyed, the genealogist and historian Elias Lychfield was commissioned to visit every parish in Dorset to record, in detail, churches and churchyards. In his book, he describes the interior of the old chapel at Tyneham. It was called the chapel of St Lawrence. The Italian equivalent is San Lorenzo. It's important you read his description of the stained-glass window. He talks about the black, one-horned goat.'

She slid another sheet of paper across the table:

a photocopy of an ancient manuscript set in bold italics.

'But what's most important is that you see the ruins, Charlie, then you'll understand, properly. You'll find them by following the track we took, then going through the woodland, past the willow tree where we saw the boy, and on up the pathway. He was trying to lead us there. I see that now. Did you know that the name Tyneham in its original form was Tigeham? It means a goat enclosure.' She stopped suddenly and rubbed at her arms.

'You must be able to feel him now. He's here again. He's not just angry. He's furious.'

I could feel it: a terrible hatred building in the atmosphere. An evil that sent fear tingling deep beneath my skin like torrents of electricity. Although it was sunny outside, darkness was forming at the edges of my vision. If we continued like this, I knew the boy would become visible once again. Caroline eyed the space around her nervously.

'Why are you doing this?' I said. 'We agreed to leave it all −'

'There something I need to tell you.' The steeliness in her tone was even more unsettling than the quietness now.

'The day after we were at the pub, the Silent Lady, I found out I was pregnant. Six weeks.'

I said nothing. What could I say? A dream – our dream – finally come true, and after all this time. The child must have been conceived in Verona. I was dumbfounded. I laughed aloud into the silence.

'But⋯ that's wonderful. That changes everything. Everything.'

Caroline turned to face me, but her face was blank and void of emotion.

'You don't know what it's been like. You have no idea.'

My mind raced with elation. Finally, after all these years of waiting, being disappointed, waiting again, hoping, praying – now, finally, we could begin our lives again, with a child of our own.

'We'll get you through it. I swear, I'll be there every step of the way. We can leave this place, sell it, get away somewhere. Rent something, or buy something new straight away. Why didn't you tell me, Caroline? That's so incredible –'

'I had an abortion two days ago,' she said. 'There's a clinic in Weymouth. I made an appointment and I went through with it.'

'What?'

'They were right, Charlie. All of them. The Hawthorns, the Knights and the rest. They were trying to stop it. Just as I have. It's the right thing. He's always trying to come back. Don't you see? You have no idea. To have it inside you, growing. To feel his darkness. You feel it now, in this room, but when it's inside you··· it's unbearable. I don't expect you to understand.'

I staggered to my feet, feeling my legs quiver beneath me.

'What are you saying? That you've killed our unborn child? Is that what you're saying?'

'He was not our child.' Her voice retained the same, emotionless quality. 'I was wrong. It wasn't the Hawthorns that got inside us. It was him. The boy. He was never ours, and never should be. He is··· something else. It's wrong. It's all wrong.'

'You're insane. You're bloody insane! What have you done?'

But, even as I spoke the words, Mrs Webber's voice resurfaced in my mind. What had she said that day in Burley?

It's all wrong.

A new level of cold now fell across the kitchen. The hairs on my arms and back bristled and stood up. Caroline let out a frightened sigh and began to tremble.

My mind was a seething cauldron of rage and confusion. I reached for the table to steady myself, unable to take it all in. I could feel the anger building inside me. All those weeks, months, years and money wasted on fertility programmes: for what? For this?

I hold my head in shame, Father, for what I did next, but in that moment I could not stop myself.

I lurched across the table and grabbed Caroline's hair. She screamed as I dragged her to the floor and struck her face with a tight fist.

'Murderer!'

'Don't let him inside you,' Caroline whimpered into the silence. 'It's his rage, not yours.'

'You're mad.'

I let her slip from my grasp and she crumpled into a bony heap on the flagstones. I could already see the bulge forming over her eye where I had struck her.

'Go to the ruined chapel at Tyneham. Read Lychfield's manuscript.

The air lifted suddenly, as though normality had somehow found its way back to this small corner of Dorset.

'All of my ancestors are cursed. It's been that way from the beginning. It'll be that way until the end. He chose us because he believes one of us will let him live, that one of us will be willing. I've done the right thing, Charlie, whatever you say.'

Then she smiled, just a small suggestion of a smile about her lips, and the stained-glass window of San Lorenzo resurfaced in my mind: the woman, holding the death's head, smiling gently back at me.

Grabbing the papers and Caroline's car keys from the table, I slammed the door as I went.

****

I arrived at Tyneham to find the gates locked.

A crooked sign hung from the cast-iron structure. Bold, red lettering stated: 'MILITARY FIRING RANGE – KEEP OUT,' but I had not come here simply to turn around.

Leaving the car at the top ridge, I climbed the gates and made my descent on foot, through the unkempt fields and down towards the village.

A thick fog had begun rolling in from the sea, steadily engulfing the area. Ghostly outlines of the dilapidated houses and tumbledown cottages cut through the ever-shifting greyness and were lost again. The place was utterly deserted, as I had known it would be. The muffled calling of gulls far above broke the quiet.

The sun, no more than a glowing disc, became fainter with each step I took until, finally, as I crossed the bridge and stepped onto the chalky track I had taken with Caroline all those weeks ago, it disappeared completely.

Here, there was no sound. Only my footsteps on the chalk. The distant gushing of a stream. Dark pines became visible to my right, their ragged peaks vague and insubstantial through the fog.

I was close now, surely, to the place where we had seen the boy.

Keeping a close eye on the woods, I continued until the willow came into view. Half-hidden in shadows and dwarfed by the other, taller trees, its tendrils drooped to the undergrowth. I squinted into the dimness. Mist lingered between the tree trunks like pale smoke, but now I could see the path, no more than a thin trail leading first down towards the stream, and then into the shadows, to the willow on the other side.

The woodland was utterly still. No birds sang. Only the stream below gushed through the quietness, becoming louder as I made my descent. The air was dank and redolent of rotting leaves, and, as I continued further down the slope, brambles ripped at my suit trousers. Still I went on, down towards the stream where the path became even narrower.

As I neared the bottom, I stumbled on a tree root, but then found my footing again and leapt from the muddy bank, over the stream, to the other side.

Scrambling up the incline, I forced my way to the willow tree, entering its shade through moist, dangling branches. The only sound inside was the gentle whispering of its leafy tendrils. Shadows danced on the dead leaves below. I moved around the gnarled trunk to the other side and brushed the curtain-like branches aside.

Before me, crooked steps protruded from the soil

and led up the embankment, through the trees and into the fog. Coated in dark green algae, the stones looked as old as the woodland itself. As I began my ascent, the sickly aroma of death filled the air. No flowers grew here, no plants. Leaves hung withered and lifeless from decaying branches. Hollowed tree stumps jutted from the ground like forgotten castles, and small, fractured bones and pale animal skulls littered the path ahead.

I retched into the silence. Sour bile rose in my throat, into my mouth, but I somehow managed to swallow it down again and continue.

At the top of the rise, the woodland gave way to rough, scrubby land. The air grew noticeably colder. I looked down to see hoof marks imprinted into the ground at regular intervals. Those of a horse, perhaps, or a large cow.

The fog was far thicker here, a dense, swirling mist, reducing visibility to a just few feet in any direction. I could hear the sea, muffled yet unmistakable, crashing and sucking on the shoreline nearby. Then I saw it, emerging as a pale, ghost-like entity through the whiteness. The ruined chapel.

A crumbling archway stood among jagged stones, steadily becoming more solid as I approached. I could see the remains of the cylindrical towers, now no more than decrepit circles of stone elevated above the grass on either side of the arch. The drawing of the place had been accurate. It would have been the same as San Lorenzo exactly, only on a smaller scale. I had expected to find the ruins covered with ivy, but only a small amount of long-dead creeper clung to the structure, as though nature had attempted to reclaim this place, but had failed.

I stepped beneath the archway, into what must once have been the interior of the church. Stones lay strewn and half-buried. The original walls, visible now only as a grassy outline, lay in the correct formation: a Benedictine cross.

A terrible sensation settled over me. No, more an inner realisation that I had made a dreadful mistake in coming to this forsaken place. The stench of death hung heavily in the fog. Beyond the crashing of waves, another sound sent a chill through me: a large animal, somewhere in the mist, not far from the chapel, galloping at speed, thumping at the ground, seeming to come towards me, then away again, moving in and out of the range of my perception. Then, only silence.

I turned to the archway. Swirling mist snaked around its eroded, primeval structure. Was there something there, beyond the grey? I was certain I had seen a dark movement, but now there was nothing, only the insubstantial silhouettes of jagged stones poking up out of the ground.

I turned again, to the perimeter walls. The fog had shifted slightly. Now something else was visible beyond the mounds. More stones, protruding from the earth like rotting teeth. These were different; even from a distance I could tell that they were not part of the chapel itself. They were headstones.

An inexplicable dread sank into me as I neared them. The lettering on the first stone, worn and crumbled with age, was illegible. The next headstone was rounded, very old. I could only make out one word: Tomson. The next was clearer. It rose at an angle from the ground, half-collapsed over the small mound it overlooked:

Here lyeth Daniel Tomsin
Departed this Lyfe XXVI December
Anno Dom MDXCIX
4 Yeares
Killed by His Owne

Next to it, another, larger stone, inscribed in deep italics:

Here lyeth Sarah Tomsin
Bearer of Daniel
Departed this Lyfe XXVI December

Anno Dom MDXCIX
Hanged Herselfe in Guilt
Blessed is she, Saviour of Armies

I knelt and brushed dried moss from another:

Beneath thys Stone Lyeth
Mary Tomson of thys Parish
Who exchanged thys Lyfe
for the better 13 March 1618
Age of 30 Yeares
With Her lies the child, rightly Taken from Her womb
So He is Silent again

Again, the distant sound of hooves charging in the fog broke the silence. I stood and went on to the next group of dilapidated stones. Coldness entered my soul as I read the inscription on one of them:

Here lyeth John Timsin
2 yeares Olde
Died June 20 AD 1710
by His Mothers fayre Hand
Son of Angel fallen
His Owne dark Wings have
folded about Him again

And next to it, another:

Here lyeth Catherine Timsin
Carrier of John
& Saviour of Men
Died June 20 AD 1710
By her Owne fayre Hand
PREPARED BE TO FOLLOW ME

Everywhere, there were headstones from bygone decades and centuries. Each marked the burying place of a woman, and those who were unmarried all bore the same name, or a version of it: Tomsin, Tomson, Timpsin, Thomas, Tomplin, Thompson.

I came to another grave, far more recent than the others. Grass had barely grown across its surface. A single black slate rested upon it. A hand-scrawled message read:

Elizabeth Hawthorn. Née Tomsin. I will follow.

Then, finally, the last stone, set apart from the others and far older, a solid rock with only one smoothed facade. Across its surface a different language, words I did not recognise. Sharp, angular, Roman lettering. I could make out but a few words:

BESTIA, TOMAS and VERA.

Something else too, etched into the stone. The profile of a unicorn with upturned daggers on either side.

Only now, for the first time, I saw them for what they actually were: not upturned daggers, but crucifixes, inverted.

A voice whispered behind me, stopping my heart in an instant.

'Now you see.'

I turned and saw his outline through the fog, emerging steadily beneath the archway. The boy.

As he approached, almost floating through the whiteness, his sightless eyes bored into me. Withered, bluish skin stretched around his skull as he smiled. Out in the fog, something bellowed into the silence, an angry, powerful sound like the peals of thunder that herald an impending storm. The hooves began again, thumping at the ground nearby.

'Hail him,' the boy hissed. 'Father of the lost. Majesty of darkness.'

It is difficult to describe the sensation of standing there, in that moment. The world had stopped. I was alone with something timeless, hateful and ancient.

Evil, in its purest form, permeated the atmosphere, hindering my ability to breathe. I fell pathetically to my knees.

'He will rise again, through me. Yours was weak, as were they all.' He waved a small, grey hand about the gravestones in loathing. 'She could not even bear me. But my time is near. A new host is found.'

The boy's silhouette became faint and then disappeared completely into the fog.

That is all I remember. I passed out and awoke hours later, among the stones. The fog had lifted. Sunshine beat at my face. Seagulls screamed overhead, far above the breaking waves.

My first thought: Caroline. How right she had been. They had all tried to stop him, to kill the child before he grew strong. Harold Knight had been the only man to help. All the other women, marked here by their headstones, had been alone in their terrible knowledge of all that was, and all that should never be. Including, now, Caroline.

And then another, more terrible awakening as my eyes fell again on the inscriptions all around me: '*by her Owne fayre Hand'; 'exchanged thys Lyfe for the better'*…

I staggered to my feet and ran through the archway, to the edge of the incline, then down the ancient steps, and on beneath the willow and across the stream. The forgotten buildings of Tyneham stood in watchful silence as I sprinted through the empty car park and up towards the entrance, where I had left Caroline's car. Tears welled up in my eyes as I frantically turned the key in the ignition and sped towards the cottage, meandering dangerously around bends and across the centre of the road. *Please*, I begged inwardly. *Please. No.*

I parked carelessly and burst into the house, running through the downstairs rooms and shouting.

'Caroline! Where are you? Caroline!'

A brooding silence filled the house.

I lurched up the stairs, checking first our bedroom and then the guest rooms until, finally, I pushed open the bathroom door to find my beautiful Caroline hanging by a rope from the ceiling. Far away, a terrible sound echoed across the fields, a haunted, desperate moaning, filled with pain and unbearable loss which then grew suddenly deafening, filling my numbed senses. It was only much later that I realised it was my own voice.

She had been dead for some time. Her face was bloated. Her feet were swollen and blue with pooled blood. Her right eye, distended almost to the point of bursting, bulged from her lifeless face. Her blue lips were frozen in a gentle smile as she creaked back and forth in the silence. For some reason I cannot explain, I thought of the first time we had met, outside James Corcoran's house in Oxford, in the snow, and how she had smiled all those years ago.

Now this.

Wonderful Caroline. All was lost.

I will not burden you with descriptions of my grief, Father. You saw that well enough during the funeral all those weeks ago.

Don't worry, I have no intention of moving Caroline's remains from St Mary's to the hill where the chapel once sat. I cannot think of a worse place to remain in death. She has suffered enough already, as have I. Sometimes, in my nightmares, I wake among the stones and wander in the fog, searching for her. When I awake, I remember that she is gone, forever.

I have had an opportunity to search through Caroline's work now. She was right, about everything. There are no records of the chapel of St Lawrence, other than the undated line drawing of its structure and, of course, Elias Lychfield's description of its interior in 1620, shortly before its destruction in 1623, and of the stained-glass window that once sat in the southern transept:

The Window is divided into Three Lights. In the middlemost our Saviour Hangs on the Cross, and in the Compartiments of each Light are Four of the Apostles, each holding a Scrowl of Scripture. Alonge the bottom are Four more Rundles of painted Glass, and these most peculiar and unsettling Emblematical Devises represented thereon:

I. *A Woman Sitting, and a Black Unicorn resting his Head in her Lap, and these words beside:* UNICORNUS BESTIAE INCARNATIO

II. *A Boy Child standing alone in Darknesse*

III. *The same Woman, now She holds the Deaths Head and is Smilinge*

IV. *The same Woman Hanging by Neck from a Tree Branche. Still she is Smilinge. Beside her, these words:* VELIS ME SEQUI

Latin, Father. It means, 'BE PREPARED TO FOLLOW ME.'

I have considered many times the best way to 'follow'. Should I find a bridge? A cliff? Beachy Head, perhaps? Or should I simply walk into the waves and not look back? I would hang myself, but I know what it means now, to find someone that way. And so it will be pills and whisky until I am poisoned beyond repair. Just remain focused, I tell myself, just for this one, final task. Adapt. Connect. Control.

I am sorry, Father, to burden you with all this, but I keep remembering what the boy said, what he whispered in the fog: 'My time is near. A new host is found.'

I pray that, when the time is right, you will do the right thing.

Goodbye and thank you,

Charles Carter

****

CONCLUSION

Creech Lane Cottage
Creech
Isle of Purbeck
Dorset

30 January 1991

Father Henry,

Thank you for your letter and enclosure, which I have read with interest.

I understand fully your reservations in sending it to me, and also why you have decided finally to do so.

The villages surrounding Tyneham support only a very small community. Rumours travel fast here and no doubt news of my pregnancy whispered its way to your little church quickly enough. What else were you to do, knowing all you did?

Six months ago, shortly after Caroline's passing – in an attempt to retrace my sister's footsteps and understand why she ended her life – we visited Verona and stayed at the Hotel Galilei, in the very same room. During our time in the city, we chanced upon the church of San Lorenzo. Quite a place, exactly as Charles had described. He had an eye for detail. Perhaps he had some uses after all. I'm sure you can imagine how events transpired when we returned to England.

Shortly after we inherited Creech Lane Cottage from my late sister and, of course, Charles Carter, we decided to move in and make some renovations. The plasterwork in the dining room has been removed in its entirety to expose the coat of arms beneath. One's ancestry should never be hidden from view. After all, we exist only because of those who came before us. It is far older than the rest of the building. I have an idea that one of my forbearers brought it here from the ruins at Tyneham.

It is important you understand, Father Henry, that I was never the same as Caroline. I was chiselled from a far harder stone. She was my sister, but she was always weak; weaker even than her spineless husband. It seems I come from a long line of incapable females, but the change is finally here.

Armies of men could not rip this boy from my womb. Each day I feel Him grow stronger within me. His power – even now – is a wonder to behold. Soon He will be here, to awaken finally. He will grow from child to man. His time is come and I will protect Him at all costs. You have read the Book, Father, surely. Revelation 12:12:

'Therefore rejoice, ye heavens, and ye that dwell in them! Woe to the inhabitants of the earth and of the sea! For the devil has come down unto you. He is filled with fury, for he knows his time is short.'

We have commissioned the design and construction of a new stained-glass window on the cottage's south face. It is now complete. The black unicorn is there, of course, and then the boy. In the next panel there is an old woman. It is me, Father, years from now, smiling because He stands beside me, no longer a boy, but a man. Son of Angel Fallen.

For the sake of your own wellbeing, do not contact me again.

Yours most sincerely,

Sarah Andrews (née Timpson)

THE END

By the Same Author

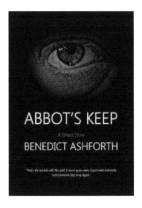

Available now on Amazon Kindle and Paperback

Praise for the ghost novella, Abbot's Keep:

'. . . the horror and suspense starts to be ratcheted up and then gradually builds up speed until the protagonists are overwhelmed in a crescendo of malevolent and inevitable evil. A really entertaining read with a delightful frisson of fear.' *Simon Ball, The Horror HotHouse*

'Ashforth does Edgar Allen Poe and Bram Stoker proud delivering a solid contribution to the literary movement. It is time that the ghost story made a comeback. With writers like Benedict Ashforth writing Abbot's Keep, a revival just might be at hand.' *Matthew J. Barbour of Horror Novel Reviews*

'Reminiscent of Poe, Abbot's Keep by Benedict Ashforth is a haunting novella with unique form and beautiful prose.' *Michael Bailey, HWA Bram Stoker Award Nominee*

'Ashforth builds on the tension and the feeling of unease with each page to revel in a wonderfully tense and unnerving finale.' *Jim Mcleod, Ginger Nuts of Horror*

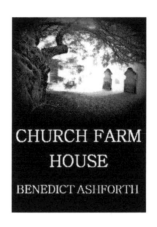

Spanning four decades, the dark history of Church Farm House is explored within four interlinking horror stories. Welcome to the nightmare . . .

Available now on Amazon Kindle

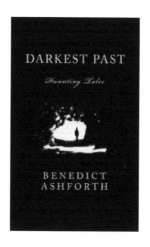

Available now on Amazon Kindle and Paperback

Five Haunting Tales from the bestselling author
of Abbot's Keep

About the Author

Benedict Ashforth lives in Dorset, England, with wife, Lynne, and son, Antony.
Benedict was born in Redhill, Surrey, and was schooled at Ampleforth College in North Yorkshire.

Follow Benedict on Twitter or email him:

@HorrorFly

benedict2012@hotmail.co.uk

Did You Enjoy VERONA?

Your feedback is immensely important to the author.

For all of your comments – positive or negative – please post your review on Amazon UK:

http://www.amazon.co.uk/Benedict-Ashforth/e/B00K7H0XZS/ref=ntt_athr_dp_pel_pop_1

Printed in Poland
by Amazon Fulfillment
Poland Sp. z o.o., Wrocław